My
Youngest,
There's
No One Like
You

Dear Mama and Papa Bear:

Do you realize that your youngest is most likely to

- have a pet name
- have tremendous people skills
- be the most natural salesperson in the family
- be good at reading a situation
- know how to get around people
- marry an oldest or only cub in a family

Did you know that most comedians are the youngest children in their families? Billy Crystal, Eddie Murphy, Goldie Hawn, Drew Carey, Jim Carrey, Martin Short, Whoopi Goldberg, Chevy Chase, Steve Martin, Ellen DeGeneres, Jon Stewart, the late John Candy, Jackie Gleason, and the father of comedy, Charlie Chaplin, are all youngest children. They are fun loving, spontaneous, and most likely to get away with way too much. Youngest children are always special because they're the littlest. They're very good at putting other people in their service. If you really want to know what's going on in a family, simply ask the baby of the family. They'll know, and they'll tell you. And as I like to say, they earn a living looking up.

Isn't it amazing how cubs all from the same den can be so different? Here's a book that will help celebrate the specialness of your youngest. Give it as a gift, or read it together to show him or her just how special he or she really is. Either way, we know you'll enjoy this book.

My Youngest, There's No One Like You

Dr. Kevin Leman
& Kevin Leman II

Illustrated by
Kevin Leman II

R Revell
Grand Rapids, Michigan

Published by Fleming H. Revell
a division of Baker Publishing Group
P.O. Box 6287, Grand Rapids, MI 49516-6287

Third printing, July 2005

Printed in the United States of America

Library of Congress Cataloging-in-Publication Data
Leman, Kevin.
    My youngest, there's no one like you / Kevin Leman and Kevin Leman II; illustrated by Kevin Leman II.
        p.   cm.
    Summary: When Youngest Cub complains that it is hard to be the youngest, Mama Bear looks at family photos with him and explains how much he means to her.
    ISBN 0-8007-1831-3 (cloth)
    [1. Youngest child—Fiction. 2. Mother and child—Fiction. 3. Photographs—Fiction. 4. Bears—Fiction.] I. Leman, Kevin, II, ill. II. Title.
PZ7.L537345Myy 2005
[E]—dc22   2004024214

To my younger sisters, Hannah and Lauren.
You're my favorites. I love you.
—Kevin Leman II

Three little cubs come out of the same den, and, oh my, are they different!

Youngest Cub ran into the den, very out of breath. Mama Bear looked up from her knitting. "What's going on, dear?"

Youngest Cub squealed to a stop. "They said you love them the best because you've been their mom longer!"

"Your cublings said that?" Mama Bear chuckled. "Oh, sweetie, never mind them. Let me get my photo album, and I'll tell you your own special story."

Mama Bear opened the big book of photos. Youngest Cub nuzzled into her neck. "Am I going to like this story?"

Mama turned the first page. "Well, let's see . . ."

You made our family
complete.

remember the day you came into this world. What a great joy that was! When Dr. Cubstable lay your wiggly little body across my tummy, you announced your arrival into this world with a big little roar!" Mama laughed out loud. "Nothing has been the same since!"

Youngest Cub giggled.

"Your arrival was a very special event."

"Was it more special than the others'?"

Mama Bear smiled.

I think your arrival was so special because you made our family complete. You were our last little one, so Papa and I could relax and enjoy you."

"I enjoy you and Papa too," Youngest Cub said earnestly.

Mama Bear laughed again. "Oh, honey. That's what I mean. You are so much fun to be around. Right from the start, you had everyone wrapped around your little paw, and you still do."

"But, Mama, the older cubs don't think I'm that much fun to be around. Sometimes they won't even let me play with them, because I'm too little. And if they do let me play, I have to be the scorekeeper!"

"Well, let's see . . ."

A natural entertainer—
even at 3:00 a.m.!

You were always good-natured, even when your sisters treated you like a living teddy bear.

"Look at this." Mama Bear pointed to a picture of the other cubs. "Trust me, my baby bear. They wouldn't know what to do without you. You were their best teddy bear. You let them dress you up in silly costumes. You played whatever they wanted to play and did whatever they asked you to do—most of the time."

Youngest Cub beamed.

"And best of all," Mama Bear went on, "you could make everyone laugh. You're our little clown who makes us all happy."

Youngest Cub nodded. "I think you love me the best."

Mama Bear tickled Youngest Cub. "Hmm, let's see . . ."

"Mr. Bear
Squash-You-All-Flat!"

You had your papa bear hooked early on. Remember when I'd send you two to the bathtub? No matter how much you didn't want to get clean, you and Papa would have fun."

Youngest Cub laughed. "Papa used to play 'Mr. Bear Squash-You-All-Flat!' He'd squeeze me into the bathtub. Then he'd splish and he'd splash until I had water up my snout . . . and I loved it!"

"See what I mean? You know, Papa was the youngest bear in his family too. You both can make a game out of anything, even bath time!"

"Is that why you love me the best?"

Mama Bear turned the page and said, "Well, let's see . . ."

The fun and
fancy-free otters
love an audience—
just like you do!

Do you notice anything peculiar about this picture?"

Youngest Cub looked at the picture of himself playing with a family of otters at the river.

"You're the only one of my cubs in it," Mama explained. "I'm sorry now that we didn't think to take more pictures of just you without your cublings. But it was hard to get you by yourself, because you liked to be the center of attention. As a matter of fact, you're a lot like these otters. They love an audience, and so do you!"

"I love the otters," Youngest Cub said. "They have fun all the time!"

"That's right. And you manage to have a grizzly's share of fun too!" Mama Bear turned the page.

"In some ways, life is easier for you than for the older cubs," Mama Bear said. "Can you guess why?"

Youngest Cub quickly answered, "Because you love me best?"

"I think it's because some of the rules Papa and I had for the older cubs didn't seem so important anymore. By the time you came along, we could just relax and enjoy you."

Youngest Cub looked at the picture Mama Bear's paw touched. "Oh, that's the time we put on a dinner show. They made me play the dog!"

"And you were the funniest dog we ever saw." Mama Bear laughed. "You hopped right into the spotlight and barked and did *everything* a dog would do!"

"Everyone laughed!" Youngest Cub recalled excitedly.

"That's right. And doggone it, you stole the show!"

Sometimes you had to
be thankful for whatever
part they'd give you!

Of all our cubs,
you like surprises
the most!

*Y*oungest Cub turned the next page. "Oh, look! Christmastime!"

"Yes," Mama Bear said. "You really like Christmas, don't you?"

Youngest Cub nodded.

"You help everyone in our family get into the holiday spirit. We all love Christmas, but so much of our joy comes from watching yours."

"Then you must love me the best. At least at Christmas!"

Mama Bear laughed again. "Well, let's see . . ."

Have I mentioned what a mischievous little cub you were?" Mama Bear put a pretend scowl on her face. "Sometimes you were a very naughty bear."

Youngest Cub didn't look worried at all. "I just like to have fun."

Mama Bear couldn't help but smile at that. "You managed to wiggle your way out of a lot of trouble. I have a feeling you've blamed your cublings for some of your shenanigans, am I right?"

Youngest Cub didn't want to admit anything and kept quiet.

"Of course, your schoolteachers aren't always as charmed as we are. I do hear from them, you know. Sometimes I think Papa and I spend more time at school than you do!"

Youngest Cub still wasn't worried. "You love me the best anyway, huh?"

"Well, let's see . . ."

Point all you want.
I know exactly who
started this!

Another meal
at the kids' table!

Your papa bear says we all have a voice inside us that says, 'I can't do that.' But he says you don't seem to have that voice. Your voice inside says, 'I'll show you!'"

Youngest Cub thought that was probably true.

"You rarely complain about being the littlest," Mama continued. "I know it's hard when you have to sit at the little cubs' table with your crazy cousins or when you have to be the one who sleeps on the floor when we go on vacation. But you are a nice, even-tempered bear, and I appreciate that."

"So do you appreciate me the best, Mama?"

Mama laughed out loud.

Oh, look at this picture of you." Mama Bear pointed to a big photo. "I remember that day. You played in the forest, and when you came home, I emptied your pockets before I did the wash. Do you know what I found?"

Youngest Cub knew, but he liked to hear it again.

"Three gross grubs, three sticky caterpillars, and a crabby crayfish! Not to mention the swarm of crickets I found under your hat!" Mama Bear chuckled. "That's another thing I really like about you—your sense of adventure."

"I know what you're trying to say, Mama."

It was hard to get
much work done with
an adventurous cub
around the house!

Mama Bear shares a special secret.

$\mathcal{Y}$oungest Cub crawled up to his mama's ear. "I like being your baby bear."

Mama whispered back, "I know sometimes you feel left out because you're too little to do what your older cublings are doing. But you're the only one who's just the right size to fit here in my lap."

"So you do love me the best?" Youngest Cub asked.

Mama Bear gave him an extra squeeze. "You'll always be a part of me, and I'll be a part of you. There's no one like you, my brave little baby bear."

Youngest Cub smiled and knew exactly what that meant. "I love you too, Mama. In fact, I'm going to stay here with you and Papa forever and ever, right?"

"Well, let's see . . ."

Youngest Cub grew
and grew until he no longer
fit in his mama's lap. But no
matter how big he got,
he was always Mama's
special baby bear.